Backbeard the Pirate

Former Captain of
The Five O'Clock Shadow

Objective

I want a job, so you'd better give me one.

Education

- Mrs. Hardscrabble's Schoolhouse
  Completed three months of first grade
  Lunchroom monitor

Honors

- First member of my class to start shaving
- First member of my class to stop shaving

Qualifications

- Hairy
- Experienced in all types of piracy
- Good at keelhauling, carousing, hornswoggling, and marooning
- Pillaging and plundering a specialty

Previous Employment

- Captain of *The Five O'Clock Shadow*
- First Mate aboard *The Black Sandwich*
- Lookout aboard *The Cackle Fruit Clipper*
- Junior Poop-Deck Swabber, First Class, on *The Jolly Boat Fluke*
- Ballast aboard the *The Grog Blossom*

References

- Sweaty McGhee, Scarlet Doubloon, and Mad Garlic Jack
- Pig

Pirate Rules

1. A pirate must look fearsome.

2. A pirate's clothes must be dirty.

3. A pirate never pays for things.

4. A pirate must wear a pirate hat.

5. Pirates do not brush their hair or teeth.

6. Pirates call each other names.

7. Pirates smell bad.

8. Pirates eat old cheese, stale bread, fish, and rats, when available.

9. Pirates are willing to fight anyone, anytime.

10. Pirates drink rum.

11. A pirate must have a parrot.

BACKBEARD

Matthew McElligott

To Justin!

Walker & Company New York

For Christy (without whose help this book never
would have been finished) and for Anthony —M. M.

First published in the United States of America in September 2007
by Walker Publishing Company, Inc., a division of Bloomsbury Publishing, Inc.
Paperback edition published in April 2011
www.bloomsburykids.com

For information about permission to reproduce selections from this book, write to
Permissions, Walker BFYR, 175 Fifth Avenue, New York, New York 10010

The Library of Congress has cataloged the hardcover edition as follows:
McElligott, Matthew.
Backbeard : pirate for hire / by Matthew McElligott.
p.   cm.
Summary: When the Pirate Council tells Backbeard that he must stop wearing colorful
clothing and look more fearsome, he decides to quit being a pirate and get a job on
shore, if only he can find work that matches his particular skills.
ISBN-13: 978-0-8027-9632-5 • ISBN-10: 0-8027-9632-X (hardcover)
ISBN-13: 978-0-8027-9633-2 • ISBN-10: 0-8027-9633-8 (reinforced)
[1. Pirates—Fiction. 2. Job hunting—Fiction. 3. Clothing and dress—Fiction.
4. Humorous stories.] I. Title. II. Title: Pirate for hire.
PZ7.M478448Bac 2007   [E]—dc22   2006102841

ISBN 978-0-8027-2265-2 (paperback)

Typeset in Post-Mediaeval and Caslon Antique
The artist used pencil, fabric, photography, and digital techniques to create the illustrations
for this book. All textures and colors throughout the book are photographs of real objects.
Book design by Nicole Gastonguay

Printed in China by C&C Offset Printing Co., Ltd., Shenzhen, Guangdong
10 9 8 7 6 5 4 3 2

All papers used by Bloomsbury Publishing, Inc., are natural, recyclable products
made from wood grown in well-managed forests. The manufacturing processes
conform to the environmental regulations of the country of origin.

This is the story of Backbeard, the hairiest pirate who ever lived.

Backbeard was also the smelliest, dirtiest, and most colorfully dressed pirate ever. How he got that way is another story, but here's all you need to know: Backbeard and his crew didn't look like any other pirates, and they were happy.

Of course, just because they were happy didn't mean they weren't real pirates. They still liked to fight and steal and smash things. They just wanted to look good doing it.

One day, while fighting, stealing, and smashing things, a cannonball landed at Backbeard's feet. Attached to the cannonball was a note.

"Pig," he sighed. "I think we may be in trouble."

That night Backbeard called the crew together.

"Listen, you stinkbottoms," he said, "I have some bad news."

"And some bad breath!" came a voice from the back.

"Button it," said Backbeard. "I've been called to appear before the Pirate Council. While I'm gone, Sweaty McGhee's in charge."

"Is it serious, Cap'n?" asked Scarlet Doubloon.

"With the Pirate Council, it's always serious," said Backbeard. "I'm leaving tonight."

At midnight, Backbeard and Pig arrived at the Isle of Bones.

Atop Skull Mountain, the Pirate Council sat waiting behind a great stone table.

"Backbeard," said Long Johns Silver, "I'll keep this brief. You look like a doofus. We don't like it."

"Crabcakes!" said Backbeard. "I thought this was serious."

"It's very serious," said Captain Kidney. "Rule number four in the Pirate's Handbook says: A pirate must wear a pirate hat."

"And rule number eleven," said Bloody Mary Mackerel. "A pirate must have a parrot."

"And rule number one," said Long Johns Silver. "A pirate must look fearsome. I've seen scarier clown fish."

"So what?" said Backbeard.

"So we're giving you a choice. Change your clothes, or we're kicking you out."

Back at the ship, Backbeard broke the news to the crew.

"They're kicking you out?" said Mad Garlic Jack. "Can they do that?"

"They're the Pirate Council," said Backbeard. "They can do whatever they want."

"But where will you go?" asked Scarlet Doubloon.

"No idea," said Backbeard.

"Will we have to change our clothes?" asked Sweaty McGhee.

"I'm afraid so," said Backbeard.

The next morning, Backbeard and Pig went to town to find a job. Soon, they came upon a man selling fish from a cart.

"I need a job!" boomed Backbeard. "Give me one."

"What can you do?" asked the man.

"Whatever I want," said Backbeard.

"I mean, what do you know about fish? And what is that smell? Is that you?"

"Probably," said Backbeard. "Or it might be the pig."

"I'm afraid I can't help you," said the man. "You're making my fish stink. Try the blacksmith next door."

At the blacksmith shop, Backbeard found a man hitting hot metal with a heavy hammer.

"What are you doing?" said Backbeard. "Give me a job."

"I'm making horseshoes," said the blacksmith. "Are you strong?"

"Blistering barnacles! I'm Backbeard!"

"I see," said the blacksmith. "Then try to hammer this metal flat. It's harder than it looks."

Backbeard took the hammer and struck the metal. The anvil and the table split in two.

"You're fired," said the blacksmith.

By the end of the day, Backbeard still hadn't found
a job.

"This is it," he said to Pig. "The last store in town.
What's a tearoom, anyway?"

"Hwuuungk," shrugged Pig.

Inside, everything was fancy and frilly. The scent of
perfume filled the air.

"This place smells more than we do," said Backbeard.
"I like it."

In the corner, he spotted a little old lady knitting.

"Such a handsome young man!" she said. "What
can I get you, dear?"

"I want a job," said Backbeard.

"Certainly! With my children gone, I can use the
help. You may start tomorrow."

The job was harder than Backbeard expected.

The first day, he broke nineteen cups and eleven saucers. He yelled at customers and made them cry. He spilled tea all over his suit.

"Don't worry, dear," said the little old lady. "Everyone makes mistakes."

By the end of the week, Backbeard was doing much better.

"I'm so proud of you, Mr. Beard," said the little old lady. "Will you do me a favor?"

"Aye," said Backbeard. "Anything."

"Tomorrow, my children are coming to visit. I'd like to leave you in charge. Here's where I'll be."

"Blimey!" said Backbeard.

The next morning, things started off well. Most of the customers got their tea. Backbeard yelled at only a few people. But by the afternoon, the shop began to get crowded.

Someone's cucumber sandwich had too much crust.

Someone's tea didn't have enough lemon.

Someone else's tea had too much lemon.

"Listen up, you jellyfish," roared Backbeard. "The next one who complains walks the plank!"

Someone threw an egg at his hat.

"Sweaty!" said Backbeard, spinning around. "Scarlet! Mad Garlic!"

"Ahoy, Cap'n!" said Sweaty McGhee.

"It's great to see you idiots," said Backbeard. "Now go away."

"You really work here?" asked Mad Garlic Jack.

"Shiver me timbers!" roared Backbeard. "Can't you see how busy I am? I said get lost!"

"We don't want to," said Scarlet. "Being a pirate is no fun since you left."

"We miss our clothes," said Mad Garlic.

"Besides, it looks like you could use our help," said Sweaty McGhee.

"Just leave it to us," said Mad Garlic Jack. "We'll take care of everything."

"You just sit and rest," said Scarlet Doubloon.

"What great pals," thought Backbeard. "I don't know when I've ever felt so proud."

That evening, Backbeard and Pig walked to the little old lady's house.

"Mr. Beard!" she said as she opened the door. "How nice of you to drop by! How are things at the shop?"

"Not good, ma'am," said Backbeard. "Everything is ruined. I'm afraid I had to fire myself."

"That's too bad," said the little old lady. "Won't you come in for a cup of tea before you go?"

"Who is it, Mother?" came a voice from inside the house.

"Mr. Beard, these are my children, Nathan, Jonathan, and Mary."
"Uh, pleased to meet you," said Nathan, Jonathan, and Mary.

"Blimey!" thought Backbeard. "I recognize those scoundrels!"

"Listen, she doesn't know we're pirates," whispered Long Johns Silver. "Will you keep our secret?"

"We'll let you be a pirate again," offered Captain Kidney.

"And wear whatever you want," said Bloody Mary Mackerel.

"And keep the pig," said Long Johns Silver.

Backbeard shrugged. "I was planning to anyway. Pass the tea."

Pirate Rules
(AMENDED)

1. A pirate must look fearsome. and/or stylish

2. A pirate's clothes ~~must~~ be dirty. may

This is good! Let's keep this. ↙

3. A pirate never pays for things.

4. A pirate must wear a ~~pirate~~ hat.

5. Pirates do not brush their hair or teeth. or backs

6. Pirates call each other names. But not in front of Mother

7. Pirates smell bad. True!

8. Pirates eat old cheese, stale bread, fish, ~~and rats~~, when available.

Also: cucumber sandwiches and assorted pastries.

9. Pirates are willing to fight anyone, anytime. *in their old clothes*

10. Pirates drink rum. *and tea*

11. A pirate must have a ~~parrot.~~ *mascot* *(pigs okay)*

Matthew McElligott

is the author of several books for children,
including *Even Monsters Need Haircuts*, *The Lion's
Share*, *Backbeard and the Birthday Suit*, and *Absolutely
Not*. Like Backbeard, he is big, messy, smelly, and
not too bright. He is very happy with his job as
a writer and illustrator because he can wear
whatever he wants while he creates pirate stories.

www.mattmcelligott.com